Care Bears™

King Funshine Bear

Written by Frances Ann Ladd

Illustrated by Jay Johnson

SCHOLASTIC INC.
New York   Toronto   London   Auckland   Sydney
Mexico City   New Delhi   Hong Kong   Buenos Aires

Designed by John Daly

ISBN 0-439-62490-8

12 11 10 9 8 7 6 5 4 3 2 1   4 5 6 7 8/0

Printed in the Singapore
First printing, November 2004

It was time for the annual Care Bear Fair in Care-a-lot.
Grumpy Bear had built a Rainbow Carousel especially
for the occasion.

But when Grumpy Bear started up the carousel,
it quickly spun out of control.

"Grumpy Bear, do something," cried the Care Bears.
"The carousel is going too fast! Make it stop!"

When the carousel finally landed, it broke into hundreds of pieces. Grumpy Bear needed some cheering up. But Funshine Bear's jokes only made matters worse.

"'Cheering up' is different than 'making fun of,'" Grumpy Bear said. "If you don't know that, maybe you don't belong in Care-a-lot anymore."

"Maybe Grumpy Bear is right," Funshine Bear said sadly. "I'd be better off in a place where no one takes anything seriously and everyone laughs all the time."

So he packed up his bag and ran away.

Before long, Funshine Bear came across a funny-looking car in the middle of the woods. When Funshine Bear sat in the car, it lifted up into the air and took him on a wild ride.

"W-h-o-o-a-a-h!" shouted Funshine Bear.

Just as quickly as the car took off, it landed with a THUD!

"Are you okay?" asked a little pig.
"I think so. Where am I?" asked Funshine Bear.
"You're in Joke-a-lot. My name's Gig," said the pig.

Suddenly, Funshine Bear was surrounded by guards.
"What's going on here?" asked a rat named Funnybone.
"This stranger is not wearing funny face makeup," said the
guard. "We're going to lock him up."

"Wait!" Funnybone shouted. "Don't you know who this is?
He's the long-lost King of Joke-a-lot. He's got the
royal birthmark."

"The ancient legend says that a bear shall fall from the sky, and upon his tummy shall be a happy, smiling sun, and the people will have a new king," said Funnybone.

Funshine Bear smiled. "That's just what happened. I'm a KING!"
"LONG LIVE KING FUNSHINE BEAR!" chanted the people
of Joke-a-lot.

"Flies!" shouted Funnybone.

"Yes, Oh Devious One," answered the flies.

"Of course, you know I made up all that king stuff,"
said Funnybone. "But when Funshine Bear is crowned king,
I can get the magic scepter and steal the royal jewels
of Joke-a-lot."

Funshine Bear enjoyed a wonderful day in Joke-a-lot. "Well, Almost-King Funshine Bear? What do you think of our little town?" asked Funnybone.

"It's perfect!" said Funshine Bear. "I just wish the Care Bears could see me now."

Meanwhile back in Care-a-lot, a group of Care Bears left to find Funshine Bear so that they could ask him to come back home. They soon found his trail.

Just as the coronation ceremony was about to begin,
the Care Bears landed in Joke-a-lot.
"Oh, this is your funniest joke ever," said Tenderheart
Bear when Funshine Bear told them he was king.

"But now it's time for you to come home with us."
Only Funshine Bear didn't know if he wanted to stay
in Joke-a-lot or go home to Care-a-lot.

"I like being king, but I really don't feel like a king,"
Funshine Bear said as he walked through the castle.

Suddenly, Funshine Bear slipped on a banana peel.
 KERSPLAT!—he fell right into the giant royal cake. Everybody laughed and laughed.
"Ha-ha! That was funny," Funshine Bear said. "But can someone help me out of this cake?"

"You're all so busy laughing that you didn't see I needed help!" yelled Funshine Bear.
"It's good to have fun, but it's also important to listen to others and think about their feelings."

At that moment, Funshine Bear made up his mind to go home to Care-a-lot.

"As long as I've got my friends, I'll always be a king," he said.

Suddenly Funshine Bear heard a cry for help.
"Funnybone stole the royal jewels!" cried Gig.

Funshine Bear ran to find Grumpy Bear and the new carousel that he had built for the Joke-a-lot Laff-fest.

Funshine Bear told Grumpy Bear to readjust the carousel.
Just like before, the carousel spun out of control and crashed into
Funnybone's hot-air balloon.

"Sir Funnybone, why did you do it?" asked Funshine Bear.

"My real name is Ratbone. I came to Joke-a-lot years ago from No-Fun Atoll," Funnybone said. "I wanted the royal jewels so my people would laugh again."

"I'm sorry I made up the story about Funshine's tummy symbol," Funnybone said. "The real royal birthmark is a smiley face." Gig looked down at her tummy. "Like this one?" she asked.

"Gig, you're the real princess of Joke-a-lot," cried
Funshine Bear happily. "I'm not the king, I'm just ME!"

After Gig was crowned princess, Funshine Bear
suggested the Care Bears take Funnybone's people back
to their Care Bear Fair to cheer them up.

"But how will we get there?" wondered Funnybone.
"I wish I knew," grumbled Grumpy Bear.

"Sometimes a wish is all it takes," cried Wish Bear.